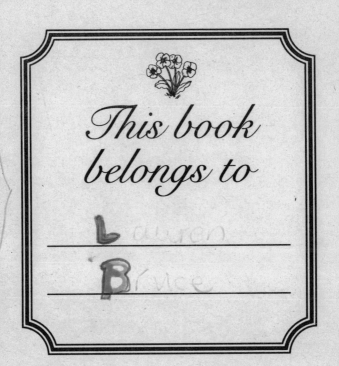

This book
belongs to

Lauren

Bruce

The Friendly Pig

AND OTHER FARMYARD STORIES

The Friendly Pig

AND OTHER FARMYARD STORIES

PARRAGON

First published in Great Britain in 1998 by
Parragon
13 Whiteladies Road
Clifton
Bristol BS8 1PB

ISBN 0 75252-532-8

Printed in Great Britain

Reprinted in 1999

Produced by Nicola Baxter
PO Box 71
Diss Norfolk IP22 2DT

Stories by Nicola Baxter
Designed by Amanda Hawkes
Text illustrations by Duncan Gutteridge
Cover illustration by Alisa Tingley

Contents

The Friendly Pig

Once upon a time, there was a very friendly pig. Now many pigs are friendly in their way. They will nuzzle your legs if you go into their sty, and sometimes they will nibble your trousers, which is rather annoying. But this particular pig, called Pongo, was very friendly to everyone. And this turned out to be rather a problem.

Pongo was given his name by the farmer's daughter, when her father returned from market with him early one morning. "We'll call him Pongo," she giggled, as the new pig was put into his sty, "because pigs are so smelly!"

"They're *not* smelly," protested her father, who had a soft spot for pigs. "It's only that they are sometimes fed smelly food."

"And what comes out the other end of them isn't exactly perfumed," laughed his wife.

"I really don't think," said the poor farmer, going rather pink, "that this is a suitable subject for the breakfast table. Eat up your crispies, Rosie."

But the name of the new pig stuck, and he was Pongo from that day to this.

On the first day, the farmer put Pongo in a beautiful new sty, with lots of straw, a big trough of water and some delicious pig nuts to munch.

Pongo strolled around his new home, which did not take long. He rolled around in the straw for a while, and found it pleasantly scratchy on his back. He had a drink of water, and found it cool and refreshing. He had a quick snack of pig nuts, and found them very tasty. Then he rubbed his back against the wall and looked around.

The sty was certainly spacious. Several pigs could have made a happy home there. But Pongo was not happy. There was something missing. Yes, there was definitely something very important missing.

Now you might think that Pongo had everything a pig could wish for, but you would be wrong. As I mentioned before, Pongo was a friendly pig. He had looked all the way round his sty and there was no doubt in his mind. It didn't contain a friend.

Pongo never was a pig to let the straw settle under his feet. He wiggled his snout at the catch on the gate and found that it might be tricky for a foolish human being to undo, but it was child's play for a pig. In no time at all, he was trotting happily off into the yard to find someone friendly to talk to.

The first animal that Pongo met was a bustling hen.

"Good morning," said the pig politely. "Pongo's the name."

"Henrietta Hen," squawked the feathery fowl. "Pleased to meet you, I'm sure."

Pongo gave a big smile. He had made a friend already.

"And I'm pleased to meet you," he said. "I knew a very nice hen back at my last farm. I'm sure you and I can be great friends."

Maybe so, maybe not," squawked Henrietta, "but just at the moment, I haven't time to stop. I've got six little chicks in a hen coop the size of a shoebox, and it's almost time I laid some more eggs. Where everyone is going to fit in, I don't know."

"May I make a suggestion?" snuffled Pongo. "I've a beautiful sty, far too large for a bachelor pig like myself. There is straw for a nest and a trough of water and even some quite tasty snacks. Why not make yourself at home there? Your family would like it, I'm sure."

Henrietta Hen cocked her head on one side. Live in a pigsty? Well, it was better than a shoebox, she supposed.

"I'm much obliged to you, Pongo," she said briskly. "We'll move in this morning. But I hope you won't mind me mentioning something…"

"Anything, dear lady!"

"Well, you will be careful, won't you, where you put your trotters when my new eggs are laid?"

"Don't give it a moment's thought," said Pongo. "I was winner of the pig polka prize on my last farm two years running. You will find my footwork as dainty as any you have seen."

Pongo wandered happily across the farmyard. Not only had he made a friend, but he had found a whole family to share his sty. What could be more delightful than that?

The next animal that Pongo met was Gobbles the goat. He was tethered by a long chain to one side of the barn. He could reach a trough of food and one of water, but he couldn't reach any of the very beautiful flowers in the garden next to the farmhouse.

"Greetings!" called Pongo. "Allow me to introduce myself. Pongo's the name. Pongo by name but not by nature! Ha ha!"

"My name is Gobbles," said the goat with a giggle. "Gobbles by name *and* by nature, I'm afraid."

"Is that, excuse my mentioning it," said Pongo politely, "the reason for the chain?"

"It is," said Gobbles. "There was an unfortunate incident with some washing. Who would think that humans could be so finicky about their clothes? I mean, why do they need *two* legs in a pair of trousers? They would stay on perfectly well with just one."

"Well, but they do have two legs themselves," said Pongo reasonably. "I know it's very unfortunate for them not to have four legs like us, and perhaps we shouldn't mention it, but you can understand how, having only two legs, they might like to cover them up."

"I suppose so," said the goat. "But did you know that humans are lopsided?"

"Lopsided?"

"Yes, they have to have special boots because their feet are different shapes. Even the two feet they do have are not the same, you see."

"I didn't know that," said Pongo. "How did you find it out?"

"There were four wellington boots standing outside the back door," explained Gobbles, "and I, well, I had a little chew at a couple of them. I thought that would be fine, because no human can wear more than two boots at once, after all. But it seems I nibbled the wrong two boots. The two that were left were for the same foot. Now I'm stuck here at the end of this chain, and I'm not very happy, as you can well imagine."

"Would you promise," said Pongo, "on your honour as a goat, not to eat washing or boots if I undid your chain?"

"I would certainly promise that, and I would be your friend for life," said Gobbles, eyeing the flowers around the farmhouse.

Of course, when he heard that, Pongo didn't hesitate. He wiggled his snout and rattled the chain until it was undone. Then he trotted off happily to make another new friend.

Primrose the cat was lazily sleeping on a sunny wall when Pongo walked by. The pig cleared his throat politely.

"Good morning," he said. "I'm Pongo, and I'm glad to see you enjoying yourself this fine and friendly morning."

The cat rubbed her paws across her eyes. "I'm pleased to meet you," she said. "But it is not a fine morning by any means. The farmer has just told me that he will sell me if I don't catch more mice."

"That's dreadful," said Pongo. "Could I help at all?"

Primrose tried to summon up a picture of a pig catching a mouse, but it seemed very, very unlikely.

"I don't think so," said the cat, jumping down to a bowl of milk

that had been left for her on the grass below.

"Why does the farmer want you to catch the mice?" asked Pongo, curiously.

"Because they eat the corn in the barn," said Primrose with a large yawn. "I thought everyone knew that."

"So if we could persuade them to eat something else," asked Pongo, "the farmer would be happier with you?"

"I suppose so," Primrose agreed, "but I don't see how such a thing could be done."

"Just leave it to me," said Pongo. "I'm quite good at talking to mice. There were a lot of them on my last farm."

So Pongo wiggled his snout and undid the latch on the barn. Sure enough, inside there were hundreds of sacks of corn. There were also hundreds of mice!

"Pongo's the name. Could I have a word?" called the friendly pig.

Half an hour later, Pongo and the mice had finished a most satisfactory chat. A few minutes after that, he accompanied the mice to the back of the farmhouse and used his famous snout-wiggling technique to open the pantry window. Then he strolled off back to the farmyard, happy to have made yet more new friends.

On the way, he introduced himself to Horace the horse, who was looking wistfully out of his stable at the lively goings-on in the farmyard.

"I wish *I* could go into your sty," said the horse, although there really would not have been room for him. "I wish I could go anywhere at all, but I just have to stay here all day. I really can't remember the last time one of the children took me for a ride."

"Why not come for a bit of a stroll with me?" asked Pongo. "It's such a friendly farmyard out here."

"But I can't get out," explained Horace sadly.

Pongo had a careful look at the bolts on the stable. "No problem," he said.

The farmer was in a hurry when he rushed in for his lunch,

but as he sat down, one or two odd things that he had only half noticed on his way across the farmyard began to creep into his tired mind.

"There are hens in the pigsty," he said slowly, "and they're eating the pig nuts."

A foolish face smiled at him from the window.

"There's a goat in the flower-bed," cried the farmer, running out of the farmhouse, "and he's eating my petunias!"

He raced across the yard, pulling on his coat as he went.

"There's a horse in the barn, and he's eating my corn!" he

cried, diving back towards the house again.

At the doorway, he collided with his wife.

"There are mice in my pantry, and they're eating my pies!" she shouted, as the force of the collision swept them both into the farmhouse.

"And there's a pig in my parlour, and he's eating my dinner!" The farmer collapsed into a chair.

"Good afternoon," said Pongo. "We didn't have much of a chance for a chat this morning. How are things going this very fine day?"

You may not be surprised to learn that Pongo the friendly pig no longer lives on the farm. After quite a lot of muttering about chops and chitterlings, the farmer took him to a children's farm, where Pongo is in his element. All day long, he makes new friends and chats with his neighbours. And the latch on his pen is extra-specially-wiggly-snout-proof!

The
Baby Boom

It was springtime. Wherever you looked on Appletree Farm there were babies.

The big tabby cat that lazed in the sunshine on the roof of the pigsty had four fluffy little kittens.

The sheepdog that spent all year nipping at the heels of the slowest sheep had five lively black and white puppies.

Down on the pond, Daisy Duck swam proudly at the head of ten fluffy little yellow ducklings.

Over at the hen coop, Henrietta Hen had five little chicks, who pecked in the dirt beside her.

Every sheep had a little leaping lamb – and some had

two. Every cow had a calf wobbling along beside her.

Even the farmer's wife, who had been rather tired for the past few months, produced twins, much to the delight of the farmer, who did a jig in the yard in his wellingtons and pyjamas.

Everywhere you looked, there were cuddly little babies and contented, if sleepy, mammas.

Only Horace the horse was feeling unhappy.

"Why haven't I had a baby?" he asked Gobbles the goat.

"Well, Horace," said Gobbles with a giggle, "you can't have a baby, you know. You see, you're a he-horse, not a she-horse."

"So?" said Horace.

"Well, chaps like us don't have babies. That's a job for, you know, *girls*."

"I don't see why," said Horace. "I'd make a very good mother."

"You'd make a lovely mother," Gobbles agreed, "but it just can't be, Horace, and you must stop thinking about it."

But Horace couldn't stop thinking about it. All around him, proud mothers were showing off their babies. And Horace's stable seemed empty and cold.

Horace became sadder and sadder. His old head drooped over his door, as the harrassed mothers and their broods bustled past.

Then, one day, Gobbles overheard Henrietta and Daisy exchanging a few clucks and quacks behind the hen coop.

"I'm rushed off my feet morning, noon and night," said Henrietta. "I don't have a moment to myself. What I wouldn't give for five minutes to put my feet up, much as I love my little chicks."

"I know just what you mean," replied Daisy. "I'm on the go all the time, too. On the pond. Off the pond. Into the reeds. Out of the reeds. And they're not safe to be left, oh no. Only yesterday, the smallest one tried to climb up a drainpipe. Imagine! I'm so tired, my wings are wobbling."

Gobbles crept away and gave the discussion some thought. Then he hurried along to Horace and leaned casually against the stable door.

"How are you, Horace?" he asked, cheerfully.

"So, so," said Horace, his face looking even longer than usual. "I'm still not a mother, you know."

"I know, Horace," said Gobbles firmly. "We've discussed that, you know. But have you ever considered babysitting?"

"Babysitting?"

"Yes, babysitting."

Horace looked confused. "Sitting on babies? Won't it hurt them?"

"No, no," cried Gobbles. "What a sheltered life you've led, Horace. Babysitting means looking after babies while their parents have a rest or go out for the evening or something. You have to be just as careful as a mother, but only for a little while."

Horace shifted from hoof to hoof. He began to look interested.

"Would anyone *want* me to be a babysitter?" he asked.

"I think they would," said the goat. "And I will help you to write a notice to put behind the barn, where the farmer won't see it."

This is what Gobbles wrote:

Babysitting service offered.

Chicks and ducklings a speciality.

Reliable horse. References available.

Horace read it, swinging his great head. "But I haven't got any references," he said.

"Well, I've written a couple for you," said Gobbles. "One is what the farmer would have written for you if he had had time. It says, 'Horace has taken my children for rides for many years. He has always been very careful and steady. Signed, the Farmer.' The other one is from me. It says, 'When I first came to the farm, I was only a little goat. Horace looked after me until I could take care of myself. I would not hesitate to recommend him. Signed, Gobbles the Goat.' What do you think?"

Horace was touched. He had to clear his throat before speaking.

"That's very decent of you, Gobbles," he said, in a husky voice. "I'll do my best not to let you down."

"I know you will," said Gobbles. "Now, I'll go and pin this up, and you can wait for customers."

There was a flurrying and a scurrying in the farmyard when Horace's notice went up. Before he knew what was happening, the huge horse had a queue stretching from his stable door all the way back to the duck pond. Within half an hour, he was booked solid for a fortnight, and at least two of the sheep had enquired whether he was thinking of offering a full-time nanny service.

So if you should happen to visit Appletree Farm, don't be surprised if you see a large horse with ten little ducklings on his back. And if you peer into

Horace's stable, you are just as likely to see two fluffy lambs playing leaplamb over his head as you are to find five playful puppies pulling at his ears.

As for Horace, he has never been happier.

"I still think I'd be a good mother," he says to Gobbles sometimes.

"Oh, Horace, don't let's go through all that again," says the goat. "After all, you make an absolutely *lovely* aunty."

Ask Mr
Muggles

The farmer shook his head. "I don't know, Sarah," he said to his little daughter. "A pony would be expensive. Someone would have to feed it and look after it. There would be bills for food and shoes. Farriers don't come cheap, you know."

"What's a farrier?" asked Sarah.

"Someone who comes round and shoes horses," said the farmer, "and who has to be paid. Who would do that?"

"Well, perhaps I could save up my pocket money," pleaded Sarah. She wanted a pony *so* badly, and the farmhouse was surrounded by lovely meadows where it could live during the fine weather.

"It would cost more than that, my love," said the farmer.

"Well, maybe I could help out more on the farm?" suggested Sarah. "You could pay me for the jobs I did."

"And when are you going to find time to do more work *and* look after a pony?" asked her father gently. "It's not as easy as you think, sweetheart."

Sarah sighed. "So you won't even think about it?" she asked.

"I didn't say that," said the farmer. "I will think about it, and better than that, I'll ask Mr

Muggles what he thinks. He often has some bright ideas about how to manage things."

"Who's Mr Muggles?" asked Sarah. "Is he the bank manager?"

The farmer laughed. "Not exactly," he said, "but he's often just as important to me. I'll introduce you to Mr Muggles some other time. Now I must get back to work."

With that, the farmer got up from the table and put on his hat.

"I'll be back around seven," he said to his wife. "Is that all right?"

"That will be fine, love," said Sarah's mother. "Supper's at half past. Will you be inviting Mr

Muggles to join us this evening,
or do you think it's too short
notice for him?"

Sarah noticed that her mother
had a twinkle in her eye, but she
didn't know why.

When the farmer had gone
back out to his fields, his little
girl went upstairs to look again
at her pony books and
magazines. If only she could
have a pony of her own! Eleanor
at school had one, and her father
wasn't even a farmer. He had to
rent a field from one of his
neighbours. Sarah's Dad
wouldn't have to do that. Surely
he could agree, couldn't he?

Sarah rolled on to her bed and looked up at the ceiling. Perhaps Mr Muggles, whoever he was, would think it *was* a good idea. Maybe he would persuade her father that *all* little girls who live on farms should have a pony of their own.

The more Sarah thought about Mr Muggles, the more she thought that he might be the answer to her problems. It was obvious that her father took a great deal of notice of what Mr Muggles said. If only *she* could have a word with Mr Muggles first, perhaps she could persuade him to say the right things.

Sarah sat up and put her books and magazines away. If she was to carry out her plan, she would first have to find out who Mr Muggles was and where he could be found.

Down in the kitchen, Sarah's Mum was baking.

"Do you need any help?" asked Sarah sweetly.

Her mother looked at her with a puzzled expression.

"It's not like you to come down and offer to help just like that, Sarah," she said. "Could there be any particular reason you want to get into my good books this afternoon? Now, tell me!"

Sarah tried hard to look shocked at the very idea.

"Of course not!" she said. "It's such a cold, miserable day, I just thought it would be nice to be in the kitchen, doing something warm and comforting, like baking."

"I see. Well, why don't you mix up the sugar and butter for these little cakes for me, and I'll make a start on the bread. Then we can have a cup of tea."

It *was* nice working in the warm kitchen, but of course, Sarah *did* have a reason for being there. After about ten minutes, she asked as casually as she could, "Has Dad known Mr Muggles long?"

Her mother smiled. "Oh, only a year or so," she said. "Before that, he used to talk everything over with Major Mangle."

"I've never heard of him," said Sarah. "Why doesn't Dad talk to him any more?"

"Oh," said her mother, "I'm afraid he ... er ... had a very bad accident during that dreadful storm we had a couple of years ago. It finished him off, I'm afraid."

"That's dreadful!" said Sarah. "What happened exactly?"

"Oh, it was awful," said her mother, with her head bent very low over the dough she was kneading. It almost sounded as though she was going to cry. "He was caught in the high winds and, well, when he was found, all his insides had been blown out."

Sarah had to sit down. "That's *terrible*," she said. "I didn't know that could happen to people." And she folded her arms around her tummy, as though she was afraid that her insides might be blown out at any moment. It was really a very nasty thought.

Sarah was so upset by the story about Major Mangle's insides that she almost forgot to ask anything else about Mr Muggles. But after she had had a cup of tea with her mother, she began to feel a little bit calmer and remembered what she was trying to find out.

"Does Mr Muggles live far away?" she asked her mother, still trying to sound as if she didn't mind very much what the answer was.

"No, no," came the reply. "He lives very nearby. I think your Dad often drops in on him for a chat during the day. He's a very useful chap for talking things over with. I even go to see him myself sometimes."

Sarah felt that there was not much more she could learn without showing unusual interest in this Mr Muggles. She would have to think of another plan to find out more.

When she had finished helping in the kitchen, Sarah hurried along to the sitting room, where the telephone directory was kept. She ran her finger along the list of names beginning with "M".

"Mudway, Muffet, Mugford, Muggeridge, Muhammad ... no, that was too far. There was no

one called Muggles in the
directory at all. Perhaps he
didn't have a telephone. That
would be strange. Almost
everyone that Sarah knew had a
telephone in their house, and
some had mobile phones as well
that they carried about with
them. Oh, maybe that was the
answer. Perhaps Mr Muggles *only*
had a mobile phone, so it wasn't
in the book. Sarah sighed. What
could she do now?

It was not until the next
morning that Sarah had her
Really Good Idea. She woke up
when she felt something heavy
jumping on to her bed. Opening

one sleepy eye, she was just in time to see Rags, the puppy, disappear through the door, dragging her favourite teddy bear with him.

Sarah hopped straight out of bed. "I'll have to follow him at once," she said to herself, "or I'll never know *where* Rags has put that bear."

That was it! Sarah stopped in her tracks and thought about Mr Muggles. If her father went to see him every day, all she had to do was to follow her father and see where he went. It would be easy!

In her excitement, Sarah completely forgot about Rags

and the stolen teddy bear. I am sorry to report that to this day she doesn't know where that naughty puppy has hidden the bear.

Sarah decided that there was no time to lose. Of course, by the time she was ready for breakfast, her father had already been up and working for at least a couple of hours, but Sarah reckoned that it was still much too early to make social calls, so it would be fine if she started her shadowing after she had eaten. Her father usually dropped in for a cup of tea around this time anyway.

Sure enough, there he was at the kitchen table. Sarah ate her cereal very quickly in order to be ready to start when necessary. As soon as her father stood up and put on his hat, she ran into the hall and put on her coat, but she waited until she heard the back door open before she went back into the kitchen.

At first the shadowing was easy. It was simple to dodge in and out of the buildings around the farmhouse as her father crossed the yard. Sarah's heart sank as she saw him climb on to the big blue tractor and set off down the lane, but in fact he was pulling a heavily loaded trailer, so the tractor moved very, very slowly. Sarah had no trouble keeping up with the vehicle, but she did worry a lot about her father looking in his central or side mirrors and spotting her. She ducked into the hedge whenever she could, although there always seemed to be unfortunately placed brambles whenever she decided to dive for cover. Before long, Sarah's coat was torn and her hands were muddy and scratched.

All that morning, Sarah followed her father. She could not have chosen a worse day. First it was very cold, and then it rained. By the time she followed her father inside for lunch, she was soaked and felt frozen.

It is very likely that Sarah would have given up there and then, for it was hard to leave the warm kitchen again for the icy world outside, if her father had not actually mentioned Mr Muggles at the table.

"Did you have a chance to see old Mr Muggles this morning?" her mother asked.

"No, not yet," said her husband. "I've been busy, but I thought I might see him this afternoon. I always look forward to our chats."

Sarah gritted her teeth and prepared herself to go outside

again. It would be worth it if it meant she would have her pony after all.

That afternoon, her father spent several hours clearing out one of the barns for the new herd of cattle expected in a couple of weeks. At least Sarah was able to keep dry, even if it was very boring crouching behind bales of straw all afternoon.

Finally, at about six o'clock, when it was already almost dark, her father set off down the lane, with Sarah limping along behind him. She had been attacked by pins and needles after crouching in a corner for so long.

Sarah could not work out where her father was going. It was now so dark that she could barely see him. She knew that there were no houses for miles along this lane. What was he up to?

Just as Sarah was thinking of turning back, her father opened a gate and slipped into a field. A shadowy figure was waiting there, and Sarah's Dad walked straight up to him. From her hiding place beside the gate, Sarah could not really see what was going on, but she could hear the low muttering of voices in the middle of the field. Had Dad and Mr Muggles agreed to meet out in the open on such a cold, dark evening? It seemed very strange and unlike Dad.

Sarah was so busy puzzling out the mystery that she didn't notice her father returning until he had almost reached the gate. She just managed to hide in time as he opened it and came through. As he did so, he turned and waved.

"Thank you, Mr Muggles!" he called. "You've been a great listener as always!"

Sarah did not think it would be a good idea to try to talk to Mr Muggles now. It was so dark that she might miss him in the field.

Instead, she followed her father back down the lane towards the farmhouse.

"I'll come back in the morning," she said to herself, "and look for footprints. I may be able to follow Mr Muggles to his home after all. The ground is very muddy, so there should be lots of clues."

Next morning, Sarah decided to take Rags with her. She had a vague idea about dogs following scents, although she did not really think that Rags was old enough to do anything useful.

As they walked down the lane and glimpsed the field ahead,

Sarah was astonished to see a figure standing in the middle of it, just as it had been the night before. Surely Mr Muggles was not waiting to meet Dad again this morning? This was really odd.

It was Rags who solved the mystery. With a happy bark, he bounded forward, right up to the figure in the field. Then he jumped up, over and over again, and tried to pull its hat off. Mr Muggles was not a human being at all. He was a scarecrow!

Sarah didn't know what to think. She was a little worried that her father, a grown man, walked about talking to scarecrows. In fact, she was so worried that she couldn't help raising the subject in the kitchen at lunchtime.

"I found out who Mr Muggles is," she said with a smile. "And I suppose that Major Mangle was the same kind of person, which is a relief in a way because I have been very worried about what happened to him."

"Yes, he was a scarecrow too," laughed her father. "Poor Major Mangle. He *was* a mess after that fierce storm."

"But Dad," said Sarah, "you said you were going to *talk* to Mr Muggles. You can't talk to a silly

old scarecrow. It isn't *real*."

"Oh, can't I?" asked her father. "Don't I sometimes see you talking to your teddy bear, or to young Rags here? Why do you do that if they can't talk back?"

"Well, they help me to work things out in my head," said Sarah. "It's almost as good as someone talking back. I can sort out what I really think about things."

"And that's exactly why I talk to Mr Muggles," said her father. "He helps me to work things out. Like whether you can have your own pony, for example."

Sarah's heart gave a little leap. What was her father going to say?

"I've thought long and hard about it," he said, "and I've decided that you are very young to look after a pony by yourself."

"But…" said Sarah.

"And Mum and I are too busy to help very much." her father went on.

"But…" said Sarah.

Her father hadn't finished. "If you work hard at school and at home this year, you can have a pony for your *next* birthday," he said. "Now what do you think? Do we have a deal?"

Sarah felt a sudden shock of disappointment. She had been hoping that her father would agree. But at the same time, following her Dad about in the cold and dark had made her think that it might be quite hard work looking after a pony all year round. After all, it would still need to be fed, even when it was cold and wet, or, worse still, very, very windy. (Sarah still hadn't forgotten Major Mangle!)

When Sarah spoke, her disappointment was gone and she had a twinkle in her eye. "Maybe we have a deal," she said, "but I think I must just talk it over with Mr Muggles before I decide. All right?"

The
Farmer
Wants a
Wife

Do you know the rhyme about the farmer who wants a wife?

The farmer's in his den,
The farmer's in his den,
Ee eye addy oh!
The farmer's in his den.
The farmer wants a wife,
The farmer wants a wife…

and so it goes on. Well, once there was a farm where the farmer really needed a wife – only he didn't seem to realise it.

In fact, it was the animals who first decided that Farmer William needed someone to live with him and look after him.

"He never looks very happy," said the biggest pig. "Every day he mooches about and hardly sees anyone. That's not healthy for a human being any more than it is for a pig. We've got to do something about it."

"Do you think he's ill?" asked the billy goat. "That can make people look miserable. I've noticed that."

"No," said the shy sheep, in a soft little voice. "I don't think he's ill. I think he's *lonely*, like I was when I had to stay on my own in the meadow last year. I know human beings don't always like to be in big groups like us, but I don't think they should be alone either."

"That's a good point," said the piebald pony. "He often comes and chats to me on his way back to the farmhouse. That's probably because he hasn't anyone else to talk to. You know, what he needs is a wife and a family. I wonder why he hasn't got them?"

"I think it's because he's so busy," quacked the diving duck. "He's working on the farm from morning till night. He never gets a chance to go out and meet someone nice. *We* have lots of free time, after all," and the diving duck looked coyly at the dabbling drake, who had been bringing her special weeds from the pond for a couple of weeks. "But I can't see what we can do about the farmer's free time," the diving duck went on, when the blush had faded from her feathers. "We can't do most of the work on the farm, after all. And it would look pretty strange to the farmer if we did."

The other animals agreed that the diving duck had probably hit upon the farmer's real problem. Each of them went away and had a long think about how to find the farmer a wife. Now some animals think more quickly than others, but this was quite a big problem, so it wasn't until a few weeks later that the animals got together again to talk about how they could help the farmer.

"It seems to me," said the billy goat, "that there's no way we can get the farmer to leave the farm more often. If he's to find a wife, it will have to be someone who comes to the farm. I've made a little list in my head, but I might have forgotten someone."

"Well, there's the post lady," said the piebald pony. "She's quite jolly, and she seems to like coming to the farm. She doesn't worry if her shoes get muddy like that lady delivering the telephone directories did."

"No, that's true," said the diving duck. "The post lady must certainly be on the list. And what about the egg lady?"

Twice a week, a lady in a big van came to collect the eggs from William's Farm. She was usually quite cheerful, too, and she had been heard to admire the big brown eggs that Farmer William's hens laid.

"The egg lady is another very good possibility," agreed the billy goat. "And I was thinking of the lollipop lady."

Just outside the farm entrance was a road crossing, where the lollipop lady helped the school children to cross the road twice a day. Once, when the weather was very cold, Farmer William had helped to tow her car out of a slippery patch beside the road. Ever since then, the lollipop lady had popped in every so often, bringing a fruit cake or an apple pie for the farmer.

"Yes," said the biggest pig. "I think the lollipop lady is the most likely of all, because she seems to like Farmer William a lot. What can we do to help them spend more time together?"

This was something else that needed thinking about. The animals went away for another week or two. Then the biggest pig called a meeting.

"I've had a really good idea," she said. "But it's a bit risky, and it will take some organising."

'What is it?" neighed the piebald pony. "Tell us quickly."

"Well," said the biggest pig, "we all think that the farmer needs to spend more time with one of those ladies, so that he has a chance to see how nice it would be to be married to her. I wondered if we could sort of accidentally on purpose lock them up together in the small barn one day."

At first sight, this seemed a ridiculous idea. How could such a thing be managed, and would it work? The animals were not sure. But when the pig explained what she had in mind, they began to think that it might be the answer to the problem after all.

"The only thing is," said the diving duck, "that I don't think we could do it three times. The farmer would be sure to get suspicious. We'd have to put them all in the barn with the farmer together. I know that's not ideal, but if he has to spend time with all of them at once, it will be easy for the farmer to see which one he likes best."

There was just one morning a week when the plan might work. That was on a Thursday, when the egg lady and the post lady arrived at about the same time, and the lollipop lady would just be getting ready to leave her post outside the farm gates.

On the first Thursday after their meeting, all the animals were ready. Luckily, it was a fine, sunny day, so no one was delayed.

"You know what you have to do?" the biggest pig said to the tiniest pig.

"Yes," squeaked the piglet. "I'm ready, Aunty."

"Wait for my signal," said the biggest pig, as the egg lady drew up and greeted the farmer, who had come out to meet her.

"Wait for it, wait for it…" whispered the biggest pig, as the post lady's van swept into the yard, and she got out.

"Now!" cried the biggest pig.

The tiniest pig ran across the yard as fast as his little legs would carry him, squealing at the top of his voice. Behind him ran the diving duck, quack, quack, quacking. Behind *her* galloped the piebald pony, neighing loudly.

One after the other, the tiniest pig and the diving duck and the piebald pony ran into the barn.

"What the …?" cried the farmer. "Excuse me a moment!" And he ran into the barn to see what was going on.

No sooner did Farmer William skid round the door than the biggest pig ran straight up behind him and knocked him over into a pile of bales. Then, to make quite sure he didn't escape, she sat on him (but quite gently).

"Help!" yelled the farmer. "Help! Somebody help!"

The farmer shouted so loudly that the egg lady, the post lady and even the lollilop lady all ran into the barn to help.

Quick as a flash, the billy goat lowered his head and charged at the barn doors. *Crash! Crash!* They slammed shut, and the dabbling drake flew up to push down the latch. The farmer, the egg lady, the post lady and the lollipop lady were all well and truly trapped in the barn.

Outside, the shy sheep and the billy goat discussed tactics.

"How long do you think we should leave them?" asked the shy sheep. "Would half an hour be long enough, do you think? Or an hour, perhaps?"

"Oh, no," said the goat. "We must leave them several hours at least, only the lollipop lady will have to be out in time to help the children this afternoon."

So the animals sat out in the yard all morning. They would have twiddled their thumbs if they had had thumbs to twiddle. Some of the sillier hens started to try to guess which of the ladies would marry the farmer. The favourite seemed to be the egg lady, because she had been so complimentary about their eggs, but the shy sheep favoured the post lady, and there were several votes for the lollipop lady too.

At last the clock on the church tower struck one, and the billy goat said it was time to undo the barn doors.

The animals could tell right away that the experiment had not been a success. The ladies looked furious and stalked off across the yard as if they couldn't get away fast enough.

When the farmer emerged, he had a face like thunder, and he looked very suspiciously at the latches on the barn door.

The animals had to wait for the biggest pig, who had been shut up with the humans, to tell them what had happened.

"It was a disaster," sighed the biggest pig. "You know, the small barn is not very big."

"Yes, yes," said the other animals eagerly.

"And Farmer William had been cleaning out my sty this morning."

"So what?" asked the animals.

"So the ladies said he was terribly *smelly*!"

"*What*?" cried the animals. "But that's a *lovely* smell!"

"Not to all humans, apparently," said the biggest pig. "I'm afraid Farmer William got rather upset too. He didn't like them saying he was smelly. I suppose you can understand it really."

"So you don't think the post lady, or the egg lady, or the lollipop lady will be Farmer William's wife?"

"No," said the biggest pig. "In fact, I don't think any of them will even talk to him in future. If only I hadn't had that stupid idea. Now we've managed to get rid of all three candidates at once. I'm sorry, friends."

Of course, the other animals told her not to worry at all, but they all secretly vowed not to meddle in the farmer's life again. He was not destined to be married, and that was that. They had tried and failed.

The next day, the biggest pig had a very sore leg. Perhaps it was all the running about she had done the day before. The farmer noticed it when he brought her feed that morning and at once went to telephone the vet.

The vet arrived at midday. She was new to the local practice, but she at once discovered what was wrong with the biggest pig and gave her some medicine to put it right.

"Thank you very much," said Farmer William, opening the vet's car door for her.

Next morning, Farmer William brought the biggest pig her feed as usual. He looked down at her and scratched her back.

"Oh dear," he said. "Oh dear, oh dear, oh dear. I don't like the look of that leg. I'm afraid we'll have to call the vet again."

"Whatever is the matter with him," wondered the biggest pig. "My leg is completely better this morning. I don't need the vet. Anyway, I thought she had very cold hands."

This time it was almost evening before the vet arrived.

"I'm sorry," she said to Farmer William. "I was very busy today."

Farmer William blushed and stepped carefully around a

muddy puddle in the yard.
Normally he would simply have
splashed through in his boots,
but for no reason that the
animals could see, he had
changed his clothes and put on a
smart pair of shoes instead.

"Here she is, poor old girl,"
said the farmer, looking down at
the biggest pig.

The biggest pig started to get
to her feet, anxious to show that
all was well, but she found that
the farmer was resting his knee
none too lightly on her shoulder,
so that it was impossible for her
to stand. Surely the vet would
realise that her leg was better?

But the vet was shaking her head. "Yes, this hasn't cleared up as quickly as I had hoped," she said, opening her bag. "I think I may have to come back again tomorrow to check this. In fact, it may take several visits."

"That's wonderful," said the farmer. "I mean, oh dear, poor old pig."

"Not so much of the old," said the biggest pig to herself, and she grunted to attract the farmer's attention. But Farmer William was busy looking at the vet, and the vet only had eyes for Farmer William. "But I'm the patient!" squealed the biggest pig.

It was amazing how many of the animals on William's Farm were poorly that year. Farmer William spotted problems the animals weren't even aware of. He even asked the vet to check the diving duck's twelve ducklings (for the dabbling drake had courted her most successfully). Soon the animals were fed up with being prodded and poked and bandaged.

"The sooner those two get married, the better," said the billy goat firmly.

And, of course, that's exactly what happened. Now everyone is living happily ever after down on William's Farm.

The
Hen in a
Hurry

There was a flurry of feathers and a pattering of skinny little feet, and Hannah Hen scurried round the corner of the hen coop.

"That hen is always in such a hurry," said Dora Duck. "Where is she going so fast?"

"I don't know," said Gerda Goat. "She never stops still long enough for me to ask her."

All day long, Hannah Hen rushed around, pausing only for a second to peck at the grain the farmer's wife scattered for her or to fluff up her feathers when the wind blew more keenly. Even at night, when all the other animals were sleeping peacefully, she could be heard scratching and scurrying in the hen coop. No one had ever seen her sitting still for a moment.

"It's not natural," said Gerda. "Even hens have to rest some time, and whatever is she going to do when she has eggs to sit on? How will she be able to keep still long enough?"

But Hannah never did have eggs to sit on. She laid one fine brown egg each day for the farmer, but she was quite happy for him to take it away with the other eggs. Then she would scurry off about her business.

Now one problem with the hen's busy ways was that she hardly ever had time to sit and think. In fact, she was not really in the habit of thinking at all, and that was nearly her undoing.

One springtime, a wily old fox came sniffing around the hen coop. He noticed that most of the hens were sitting comfortably in their nests, but Hannah Hen was rushing about as usual. The hens on the nests would be hard to catch, for they were safe inside the hen coop, but Hannah was out and about all day long. The hungry fox licked his lips. He loved a chicken dinner.

Next morning, when Hannah rushed around the side of the old barn, the fox was waiting.

"Where are you off to in such a hurry?" he asked. "It's a beautiful day. Why don't you stop to enjoy it, my dear?"

But the hen did not even pause to think who was talking to her.

"I can't stop," she said. "I've got much too much to do today."

"I'm sorry to have disturbed you," said the fox politely.

Next morning, the young fox was waiting again.

"Still so busy?" he asked, as Hannah scuttled around the building he was leaning against.

"Always busy," puffed Hannah, slightly out of breath. She had a vague impression that she was talking to a reddish kind of dog, and she knew that there were dogs who sometimes liked to chase chickens for fun, but she did not really feel worried.

Next morning, as she scurried on her way, Hannah was in for a surprise. The clever fox had put a big, open bag just round the corner. As Hannah came hurtling along, she ran straight into the bag. The fox quickly pulled the strings around the top of the bag, and Hannah Hen was well and truly trapped inside.

"Help!" cried Hannah. "Help! Help! Help!"

But the thick bag muffled her cries, and the fox had soon carried her far away from the farmyard and all her friends.

I'm sorry to say that the fox had very bad manners. He did not lay the table and sit down nicely for his dinner as his mother had taught him. No, he simply opened the bulging bag, stretched his jaws wide, and swallowed Hannah Hen whole.

Well, that's the end of Hannah Hen, you are saying, but you are wrong. Inside the fox's tummy, Hannah was as busy as ever. She ran up and down and tickled his tonsils. She fluffed out her feathers and kicked his ribs. And her scratchy little feet went scurrying up and down all day long.

The fox very quickly began to regret that he had caught and eaten that lively hen.

"Oooooh!" he groaned. "What is happening in my tummy?" He

could feel those skinny feet marching up and down in his insides, and he began to feel very ill indeed.

Not knowing what to do, the fox crawled off to his mother's den, stopping every now and then for a moan and a groan.

The mother fox took just one look at her son.

"What have you been eating?" she asked. "It certainly is something that should have been left on your plate."

"It was a hoppity hen," said the fox. "I caught her so cleverly, but now she is hopping up and down in my tummy, and it *hurts*."

"I'm not surprised," said his mother. "Did you sit down properly at the table and eat her like a well-brought-up little fox?"

The younger fox hung his head. The answer was plain for his mother to see.

Then his mother went to the cupboard and got out a big packet of white powder. She mixed it with some water and put it in a bowl.

The younger fox looked doubtfully at the mixture. As it sat in its bowl, it fizzled and hissed as though it was alive.

"There is only one thing to do," said the mother fox. "That hen will have to come right out of your tummy. And this mixture is the stuff to do it."

She picked up the bubbly mixture and gave it to her son. But despite the scratchy feet in his tummy, the fox hesitated.

"Go on," cried his mother, her patience now at an end. "You got into this fix in the first place by not listening to your wise old mother. You had better start now."

So the younger fox lifted the bowl and drank the white mixture down with one big gulp.

Inside the fox, the mixture bubbled and rumbled, and you have never seen a fox look so surprised as when Hannah Hen came jumping right out of his mouth. As you can imagine, her fidgety fast feet didn't stop for a moment. She was hurrying over the hill and back to the hen coop as fast as her scrawny little legs would carry her.

Well, Hannah is a changed hen now. She has raised three beautiful broods of fluffy chicks, and she is always careful to peep round corners before she hurries ahead. As for the fox, he has not been seen in the farmyard for many a long year, and I hear that his table manners have improved enormously!

The Kindly Cow

Once upon a time, there was a cow called Buttercup who could not do enough to help others. If baby animals were shivering in the winter winds, she let them snuggle down with her in the warm straw in the cowshed. If a farm animal was feeling poorly, she would trot happily off to find some fresh green dandelions and daisies to make him feel better. She was a very kindly cow, and it upset her when she wasn't able to help her fellow creatures.

In fact, as the years went by, the cow began to be rather a *worrier*. She didn't wait for animals to come to her with their problems, she tried to foresee difficulties long before they arose.

Patrick Pig was almost driven to distraction by the kindly cow's worries about his health.

"Your sty is very draughty, my friend," she said to him one day. "Won't you let me block up these cracks with some squelchy mud from the yard?"

"No, no," said Patrick Pig. "I like that draught. It keeps me cool in summer, and even in the winter it's nice to have some fresh air. I'm happy with my sty just the way it is, thank you."

But Buttercup could not let the matter alone. She was sure that the sty was not healthy. Every day for the next fortnight she trotted along to see Patrick.

"Was it you I heard coughing last night, Pat?" she asked. "Would you like me to borrow that woolly scarf from the scarecrow? It would help to keep your delicate throat warm."

"My throat isn't delicate," said Patrick. "And it wasn't me coughing last night."

Next day, the cow was back.

"Here is a mouthful of straw from my cowshed," she said. "It will help to keep your trotters off that hard, cold floor. You must take care of yourself in this chilly weather, my friend."

"That's very kind of you, Buttercup," said Patrick, "but I really don't need more straw. I have a lovely big bed in the corner, and I quite like to keep the rest of the floor clear, so that I can practise my tap dancing."

"Tap dancing! Oh, is that really wise?" Now the cow had something new to worry about.

"You're not a *small* pig, Patrick. What about the strain on your knees and ankles, not to mention your trotters? And please be careful that you don't slip."

"That's why I don't want more straw in my sty," explained Patrick patiently, but the kindly cow was now so worried she could hardly think straight.

"Never mind the straw, Patrick," she said anxiously. "I'm going to hurry off to find you some embrocation for your joints. I'm sure I saw the farmer put some away in the barn the other day."

The pig had no idea what embrocation was, but he was pretty sure it was something he didn't want. I'm afraid he trotted off to see his friend the goat, so that he was quite definitely *out* when Buttercup returned.

Of course, the other animals discussed Buttercup and how difficult she was becoming.

"It's such a shame," said the goat. "She always means well, but I find myself going out of my way to avoid her."

"I know what you mean," said Ducky Duck. "Last week she was worried that the water was too cold for my ducklings. She thought they would all catch cold in their little legs. I tried as hard as I could to explain to her that ducklings are *meant* to spend a lot of time in cold water, but she just wouldn't listen. In the end, I'm afraid we had to swim out into the middle of the pond so that she couldn't bother us any more."

As the weeks passed, Buttercup became more and more impossible. But the animals also noticed that she was becoming very tired and miserable herself. One day, Patrick Pig, who had successfully managed to avoid the dreaded embrocation, asked Buttercup whether she was feeling well.

"Oh, I'm fine, Patrick," sighed Buttercup. "Don't worry about me, please."

But her head sagged towards the ground as she spoke.

"No, no, Buttercup," insisted the pig. "You're always so anxious about *us*. Now we're worried about *you*. We can all see that you're not yourself at the moment. Please tell me what's the matter."

Buttercup looked unhappily at the pig. She was always anxious about other animals' problems, but she felt awkward talking about her own.

"It's nothing really," she said. "I'm just being a silly old cow, but the trouble is I'm not getting much sleep at the moment."

"Isn't your lovely cowshed comfortable?" asked Patrick. "It

always looks very cosy, and I have heard some of the younger animals say that it is a fine place to stay."

"Oh, how kind," said Buttercup. "No, it isn't that. My cowshed is perfect. It's just that I have so many anxious thoughts going round and round in my head, I simply can't drift off to sleep."

"What sort of anxious thoughts?" asked Patrick, although he was rather afraid he might regret asking the question.

"Oh, silly things really," said Buttercup. "I worry about whether the baby goats have nibbled the flowerbeds and

made their tummies sore. I get
concerned about the sheep and
whether they are too hot in their
woolly coats when the sun
shines. I wonder whether the
farmer has remembered to put
his winter vest on when the wind
is whistling round the farmhouse.
I think about the little birds in
their nests and get anxious about
the farm cat creeping up on
them. I worry…."

"Yes, yes, I see!" Patrick Pig felt he had to interrupt before he began to feel as anxious as poor Buttercup did.

"Don't you think, old friend," he suggested gently, "that you could leave the animals and humans concerned to worry about themselves? After all, your worries don't stop bad things happening – or good ones either, for that matter."

"I know you are right, Patrick," sighed the cow. "But those thoughts just buzz round and round in my poor old head, until I am so worried I simply *can't* get to sleep, no matter what I do."

Now Patrick really did feel worried himself, but he was a sensible pig who knew that the best thing to do with worries is to talk them over with someone else. He hurried off once again to discuss the matter with his friend the goat, and while he was there, most of the other animals came along to see what was happening. Soon everyone was trying to think of a way to help the kindly cow.

"Counting sheep is very good," said one little lamb. "That's what my mother says, and she's very clever about that kind of thing. But you do have to be able to count up to quite a high number, and I'm not sure how good cows are at counting."

"Neither am I," said Patrick, "and we don't want to give Buttercup something *else* to worry her, do we?"

"Drinking milk before bedtime is supposed to be very good for helping you to sleep," said Ducky Duck. "I wouldn't fancy it myself, but other animals like milk."

"The problem there is that the only place we can get milk from is Buttercup herself," said the goat. "That doesn't sound very sensible to me. What about exercise? I've heard that a brisk walk in the fresh air can help humans *and* animals to get a good night's sleep."

"But Buttercup gets lots of exercise," said a sensible sheep. "She is always running about to see whether we are all well and happy. I don't think more of that would help her very much."

In the end, the animals had to admit that they really did not know how to help Buttercup. And perhaps that was just as well, because the next night something happened that helped Buttercup to help herself.

The following day was cold and windy, but as the afternoon

wore on, dark storm clouds gathered over the farm. All sensible animals hurried into their cowsheds and hen coops and barns and sties. The ducks and ducklings sheltered deep in the reeds at the edge of the pond, and sheep cuddled together in the shelter of a wall.

As the first heavy drops of rain fell, the wind blew harder. It whistled round the farmyard and rattled the farmhouse windows. It banged gates and upset feed buckets. First wisps of straw danced through the restless air. Then larger objects began to be thrown about by the wind.

At the height of the storm, there came a horrible creaking sound. Louder and louder it grew, until ... *crash!* ... the huge tree that stood in the corner of the farmyard fell with a noise like thunder, just missing the pigsty.

As though it had exhausted itself with the effort of pushing over the tree, the wind suddenly dropped, and the rain stopped. One by one, the animals came cautiously out of their homes and shelters to see what the huge noise had been.

What a mess there was! The farmyard was filled with broken branches and twigs. There were broken tiles from the roof of the barn and, of course, a massive tree lying diagonally across the farmyard. It was a miracle that none of the buildings had been hit by the tree, and it was very, very lucky too that all the animals and the farmer in his farmhouse had not been harmed.

In fact, no one really seemed to have been seriously affected by the storm. At least, that was what all the animals thought until they heard a tiny twittering sound coming from the branches of the fallen tree. A little bird, who had nested in the highest branches, was trapped by a

"I have the perfect place," smiled Buttercup. "My cowshed is warm and safe. There is plenty of straw to build a nest. I would be delighted if you would come and live there."

"But is there anywhere to perch and sing?" asked the little bird. "Although it would frighten me to stand on a branch now, I would miss not being able to sing whenever I felt happy."

Buttercup looked puzzled, but Patrick gave a happy snuffle and came up with an excellent suggestion for the little bird.

"What about Buttercup's horns?" he asked. "They would

make a lovely perch for you whenever you wanted to sing. I am sure that Buttercup would be careful not to move her head too much while you were sitting and singing there."

It was the perfect solution, and the little bird agreed gratefully. But the strange thing was that Buttercup also benefited from the arrangement.

"You are looking much happier, Buttercup," said Patrick one day soon after the storm.

"Yes," said the kindly cow. "Each evening, the little bird perches on my horns and sings me to sleep. All the worries in

my head go right away when I hear her lovely song, and in the morning, I am fresh and ready to go about my business as usual."

It was true. Having a good night's sleep meant that kind Buttercup could think clearly during the day. She no longer bothered the animals with her own worries about their health and happiness, but she was always ready to help any creature who needed her. As usual, Patrick Pig put it well.

"That storm was frightening at the time," he said, "but now we are all happy. Those stormclouds certainly had silver linings!"

Mrs Field's
Flowers

Cowslip Farm was owned by Mr and Mrs Field. They worked very hard to make it the best farm in the neighbourhood. The hedges were trimmed, and the fences were mended. The animals looked happy and well looked after. There were no loose tiles on the stable roof or muddy puddles in the farmyard. It was a beautiful farm, and Mr and Mrs Field were happy living and working there, even if they were up before dawn every day.

But Mrs Field had a little dream of her own, and as the years went by, it became more and more important to her. One day, as she walked through the orchard with her husband, she decided to mention her secret wish, although she was afraid he would think she was being silly.

"Every year," she said, "we harvest the finest wheat for miles around. In the field behind the farmhouse, we grow all the vegetables we need, with some over to give to our friends and neighbours. Our hedges are full of berries in the autumn, and our apple trees are heavy with fruit."

"That's true," said her husband. "Is there something else that you think we should grow? Plums? Oats? Barley, perhaps?"

"Well, yes and no," said Mrs Field hesitantly. "What I would like to grow is not really a crop at all. It would be just for our own pleasure, not to sell."

Mr Field looked puzzled. "Did you want to plant a tree outside the farmhouse?" he asked. "I'd be quite happy about that if it was the right kind."

"No," said Mrs Field. "What I was thinking of was flowers."

"Flowers?" echoed her husband. "What sort of flowers?"

"I don't mind really," said Mrs Field shyly. "I don't want many, just a little flowerbed outside the farmhouse, perhaps where I could see it from the kitchen window. I have wanted one for such a long time, but we are always so busy, I didn't like to mention it."

Mr Field smiled. "Why ever not?" he asked. "Of course we shall have a flowerbed, my dear. You are right that it would look lovely next to the farmhouse. Why shouldn't we grow plants for fun now and again? I will start to dig the ground this afternoon when I have finished the milking."

"And I will dig too," said Mrs Field. "After all, it was my idea."

So that afternoon, Mr and Mrs Field dug a beautiful flowerbed right under the kitchen window.

"We'll have to wait until spring before we plant seeds," said the farmer, "but we can buy some at the market tomorrow."

Next day, Mr and Mrs Field set off along the winding road to the next town. All the way there, Mrs Field dreamed about the pretty flowers she would choose.

That evening, when the pair arrived home, Mrs Field had six packets of seeds in her bag. She could hardly wait to plant them the next day.

The winter passed so slowly that year! Finally, a sunny morning arrived when Mr and Mrs Field looked at each other across the breakfast table.

"Today?" asked Mrs Field hopefully, smiling at her husband.

"Today," laughed Mr Field.

That morning, Mrs Field carefully raked the plot that had been prepared and sprinkled on the seeds. Then she raked the soil gently over them and gave

them a long drink of water from
her watering can.

"Now all we have to do is
wait," she told her husband with
a smile.

But when Mrs Field came back
from cleaning out the pigs, she
cried out at the sight of her
precious little garden. Mr Field
came running, and the pair stood
and looked miserably at the hens
who were happily pecking the
seeds from the ground.

"It's not their fault," said Mrs Field. "They're only doing what chickens are meant to do. But I think we'll have to say goodbye to our beautiful garden."

Mr Field scratched his head. "Perhaps the best thing would be to wait a month or so," he said. "Then, instead of planting seeds, we could buy some little plants and put them straight into the ground. The hens won't eat them, if we choose carefully."

Once again, Mrs Field had to wait, but it was such a busy time on the farm that she did not have much time to worry about her flowerbed. When weeds began to grow on it, she carefully hoed them away, ready for the day when her new plants could be put into the ground.

When the time came, choosing the plants was even more fun than choosing the seeds had been. Mr and Mrs Field came home from market with six trays of beautiful plants. Mrs Field hurried out to plant them straight away. When she had finished, there were a lot of spaces between them, but that just meant that there was room for the little green plants to grow.

"Soon we'll have flowers under our window," said Mrs Field.

All went well for several weeks. The plants thrived under Mrs Field's tender care. Every day she watered them (but not too much) and pulled out any tiny weeds (but very gently). And each evening, when Mr Field came in from the farmyard, he smiled at his wife.

"Lots more leaves today," he would say, "and I believe some of those plants are getting ready to produce flower buds."

It was really very exciting. When the day came that the first little flower opened, Mr and Mrs Field were as happy as children with their little plot.

You can imagine how horrified the couple were to look out of their window a week later and see their flowerbed in ruins. Every plant had been nibbled and munched. Only one or two flowers remained, and the cause of the disaster sat happily in the middle of the bed, twitching his whiskers and waggling his ears.

"I don't believe it!" cried Mr Field. "Haven't rabbits got any sense at all? Just at the back of the farmhouse there are rows and rows of juicy carrots. Has that rabbit nibbled those? Oh no. He has to come hopping round here and make a snack of our beautiful flowerbed. I'm so angry, I could cry."

Mr Field would have carried on like this for several more minutes, if he had not heard a tiny sound behind him and realised that his wife really *was* crying. At once he hurried over to where she was sitting and put his arms around her.

"Don't worry, darling," he said. "We'll think of something. You *shall* have flowers, I promise."

Over the next few weeks, Mr Field asked for advice from everyone he met, but the news was not good. He heard lots of ideas for keeping rabbits away from precious plants, but none of them seemed very satisfactory. He knew that his wife would never agree to harming the rabbits, and it is difficult to enjoy beautiful flowers if they have a heavy metal cage all the way round them.

"I'm sorry, my dear," said Mr Field to his wife, "but I really don't know what to do. It seems that rabbits are very hard to keep away, and there are hardly any plants that they will not eat."

But Mrs Field was reading a countryside magazine, and she looked up with a smile on her face – the first that Mr Field had seen for some time.

"I think I have the answer," she said. "Just look at this article."

Mr Field glanced at the page his wife had been reading. He

read the heading: "Bring Back Our Wildflowers" and saw a picture of the loveliest display of flowers you have ever seen.

Over the next few weeks, Mr and Mrs Field read several books from the library and chatted with an expert who lived in the next village. They learnt that it was not just a case of planting seeds, but of treating the ground in the right way.

Straight away, Mrs Field stopped weeding her flowerbed, but let the little weeds grow and flourish. Strangely enough, the rabbits did not nibble them, although they were just as green and healthy as the flowering plants had been.

In a surprisingly short time, little starry flowers covered the bed, soon to be joined by some tiny blue blooms and an orange plant that crawled through the others and even started to climb up the white painted fence around the farmhouse.

The wildflower bed was a tremendous success. Each year after that it got better and better. Mr Field looked across the table at his happy wife.

"It's not only the wildflowers that are blooming this year, my dear," he smiled.

The
Difficult
Duck

What do ducks like to do? Well, they enjoy swimming on ponds, where they can dive and dabble and generally do duck-like things. They quite like foraging in the reeds and weeds at the edge of ponds too, and they are often quite happy to gobble up bread thrown to them by passing humans. Those are the things that ducks like to do, aren't they?

Not when it comes to Daphne Duck, they're not.

Daphne really is the most difficult duck you have ever met. She lives on Five Meadows Farm, where she regularly drives the farmer to distraction. Let me explain what she is like.

Now most farmers, as you know, get up very early in the morning. The little birds that sing the dawn chorus while it is still dark have barely started their practice scales when most farmers are hopping out of bed. But have you ever heard of a *duck* joining the dawn chorus? You've guessed it. Daphne does. At three o'clock in the morning, when even farmers are usually in their beds, Daphne sits on the bathroom windowsill of the farmhouse and begins the loudest quacking you have ever heard.

Every morning, the farmer wakes with a start, for his bedroom is right next to the bathroom, and, I'm afraid, he mutters several rather rude words before he pulls the pillow over his head and tries to get half an hour's sleep. Even through several thousand feathers, it is surprisingly easy to hear the loud quack of Daphne Duck. It is also surprisingly difficult to go back to sleep after being woken by an alarm duck. Somehow that quacking sound seems to echo in his head.

Outside the farmhouse of Five Meadows Farm, there is a

beautiful duck pond. It is fringed with reeds and filled with fish. On the lily pads in the middle, several little green frogs croak and hop. No duck could wish for a finer home.

But will Daphne deign to live on the perfect pond? Oh no. She makes a nuisance of herself waddling round the farmyard, bouncing first into the pig's water trough and then into the horse's. In fact, all the animals are fed up with having Daphne's muddy feet paddling in their water, but it seems impossible to stop her. Even when the pig grunts, and the horse snorts at her, Daphne pays no attention to either of them.

"What's a little mud between friends?" she quacks. "It's lovely, healthy stuff. Everyone should eat a little mud every day."

Of course, Daphne was quite wrong about that, as she was about most things, so I don't want to hear that you have been munching mud, all right?

Most ducks eat pondweed and fish and other watery delicacies. Daphne's diet, of course, was quite different. That duck liked apples. Yes, round, ripe apples were her favourite food, and she didn't mind where she stole them from. The farmer's fruit bowl was often raided, whenever he foolishly forgot to close the kitchen window.

Of course, it is not natural for ducks to eat apples. Their beaks are not built for it. But Daphne seemed to manage very well. She munched the ripe fruits, core and all, and seemed to thrive on them. Indeed, no other duck had such glossy plumage.

I expect you are wondering why the farmer bothered to keep this troublesome bird. More than once, his wife found her eyes straying through the duck recipes in her largest cookery book. And the farmer often dreamed he could smell the delicious aroma of *duck à l'orange* – especially at three o'clock in the morning.

But in their heart of hearts, neither the farmer nor his wife could forget that Daphne was also the best guard dog they had ever kept!

On the night when the chicken thieves crept into the yard,

Daphne not only woke the
farmer but pecked one of the
thieves so badly on the nose that
it has looked strangely like a
beak ever since (and the police
had very little difficulty in
spotting the culprit later the
same night).

When a boy drove one of the
farmer's tractors right out of the
yard just to prove that he could,
Daphne sat herself firmly on his

head and wouldn't get off until his mother arrived to take him home and send him to bed without any supper.

But it was with the apple-stealers that Daphne really excelled herself. She attacked them so furiously that every single one of the gang thought that a whole flock of geese had been let loose in the orchard. Of course, it was night, so they could not see that a solitary duck on a mission dear to her heart was pecking their knees and flapping her wings in their faces. Although the apple-stealers were never caught, not

one of them ever troubled the farmer again.

So that is why Daphne does not now need to splash in the animals' water troughs (though she sometimes still does), or steal the apples from the farmer's kitchen (though she sometimes still does), for she has her own bowl of water in the orchard and as many apples as she can eat (which is a lot). Each spring, she brings up a brood of ducklings under the blossom-laden boughs.

And at three o'clock in the morning? The farmer has bought double-strength earplugs and sleeps with a smile on his face.

The Farmhouse Mouse

When Farmer Brown had to fill in forms about who lived in the farmhouse at Daffodil Farm, this is what he put:

David James Brown, 43 years

Megan Sarah Brown, 40 years

Matthew James Brown, 14 years

Peter David Brown, 14 years

Eleanor Jane Brown, 10 years

Ben (sheepdog), 9 years

Carla (cat), 7 years

Barley (cat), 6 years

Ruffles (guinea pig), 2 years

Bubbles (goldfish), 1 year

Mouse (mouse), who knows?

Perhaps you can tell from this list that of all the animals and people who lived with the farmer and his wife, only one gave him sleepless nights and anxious days. It was that wretched little mouse, who lived somewhere in the walls, or up in the attic, or under the floorboards, and who crept out almost every night and nibbled something or other in the farmhouse kitchen.

At night, the farmer lay awake and felt sure he could hear the pattering of tiny feet tiptapping down the stairs. Many times he had crept out of bed in his pyjamas and felt his way down into the kitchen without turning the light on, determined to catch that annoying little creature as it helped itself to yet another piece of pie or chunk of cheese.

But the farmer never so much as glimpsed a tiny twirly tail disappearing around a corner. Instead, he twice stubbed his toe on the hall table and once banged his nose *very* hard on a grandfather clock that he had forgotten was there.

There was no doubt about it. That mouse was just too clever for Farmer Brown, and although he tried to persuade all his family to help him catch the little scamperer, it was too clever for Mrs Brown, or the twins, or

Eleanor, or the dog, or the cats, or the hamster, or even the goldfish (although to be fair, as he could not leave his bowl, it would have been hard for him to help with this important project).

But, you will be asking, what *about* those cats? Isn't that one of the reasons that farmers keep cats – to catch mice? Well, when it came to catching mice, those cats were worse than useless. Carla was a great big fluffy white cat, so fat that she could hardly move. No self-respecting mouse would have been caught by Carla because you could hear her wheezing half a house away as she waddled towards you. Barley was not much better. He was a daredevil cat, and his exploits always ended in disaster. Barley was not content to sit quietly by a mouse-hole, waiting for its little occupant to emerge. Oh no. Barley had to climb up on to a cupboard on the opposite wall, ready to make a death-defying leap if he saw so much as a twitching whisker. Barley's leaps were famous in the farmhouse, because he hardly ever leapt alone. Sometimes it was saucepans, sometimes crockery, sometimes bags of flour that came crashing to the ground with him. By the time Barley had picked himself up and dusted himself down, any twitching whiskers had long since disappeared. The cats also put paid to the farmer's attempts to catch the mouse in a trap. First Carla, clumsily wandering into the kitchen, caught her fluffy tail in the trap and set up such a wailing that the whole house was woken. Then Barley, leaping from the table, jumped straight into the trap. He had sore toes for a month, which made his leaps even more destructive than before.

So the cats were no help at all, and the farmer regularly made threats to send them to the cats' home and buy a certified mouser who would rid him of the cheeky little pest once and for all.

Now I will tell you the real reason why the farmer never catches the farmhouse mouse, but you must promise never to tell him. *It's because there isn't one at all.* The pieces of pie, the chunks of cheese, the nibbles of this and that all go straight into the tummies of the dog, the cats, the hamster and even the goldfish. *They're* not going to tell the farmer that there are only ten inhabitants in the farmhouse. Are you?

Too Many Cats!

How many cats would you say were *too* many? Four? Six? Ten? Twenty-four? Mrs Martin, who lived at Maple Farm with her two daughters, *loved* cats. There were thirty-six of them on the farm, and she knew them all by name.

It had all started with two little kittens called Moppet and Poppet. After a couple of years, Moppet had four little kittens. After another couple of years, those kittens had kittens of their own, and so it went on. And as well as the cats that were born on Maple Farm, others came to visit and simply never seemed to

go back to their own homes
again. Mrs Martin counted them
as permanent visitors.

One day the Government Vet
came to call. He was happy with
the contented pigs and the healthy
cows. He approved of the way
Mrs Martin was looking after her
sheep and goats. He even gave a
clean bill of health to the hens,
ducks and geese. But when it
came to cats, he drew the line.

"You have too many cats on
the farm, Mrs Martin," he said.
"Some of them will have to go."

"How many is too many?"
asked Mrs Martin, just as I asked
you at the beginning of the story.

"Shall we say that half of them must go?" suggested the vet. "I expect it to be done by the next time I call, in a month's time."

Mrs Martin went back into the farmhouse with her mouth set in a severe line. She poured herself a cup of tea and sat down in her chair with a *thump*.

"I'm not doing it," she said. "There is plenty of room on this farm for my cats – and more too if they arrive. They are all well fed and happy. Why should I get rid of any of them? And anyway, which ones would I choose? The old cats who have never known another home? Or the young ones who still need their mothers?"

Mrs Martin's daughters tried to persuade her to be sensible.

"That man can make you close down the farm, if you don't do as he says," they protested. "Can't you find good homes for some of the cats?"

"Good homes?" cried Mrs Martin. "Half of those cats came here because they were unhappy in their own homes. I can't send them out to people who may not take care of them. Do you think that's the kind of person I am? No, those cats are staying here."

Still, as the weeks passed, Mrs Martin did begin to feel a little

worried. Would the Government Vet really close down her farm? As the day of the next inspection drew near, all kinds of wild ideas passed through her mind. Could she hide half the cats until he was gone? Could she give him some of her cowslip wine, so that he wouldn't be able to count properly? Could she pretend to be ill and ask for more time? None of these ideas seemed very helpful.

The day of the Government Vet's visit dawned sunny and warm. Everywhere you looked around the farmyard there were cats lying in the sun or delicately licking their paws. It was the worst possible day for a cat count.

The Government Vet had a clipboard and a calculator. The Government Vet had sharp little eyes behind shiny spectacles. He spent two hours walking around the farm, making notes as he went.

When he arrived back at the farmhouse, Mrs Martin was waiting for him with a cup of tea.

"Thank you," said the G.V. "I needed that. Now, Mrs Martin, I have done a thorough count, and I find that you have exactly thirty-six cats. Does that agree with your figures?"

"Yes," said Mrs Martin faintly.

"Now," said the G.V., "I didn't do a full count before, so how many cats were there last time I called at Maple Farm?"

Mrs Martin crossed her fingers behind her back and suppressed a desire to giggle. It was going to be all right. She looked the Government Vet squarely in the eye and said without a blush, "Sir, there were seventy-two."

The Carrot
Crop

Now it is a strange thing about farming that no two years are ever the same. One year oats will grow beautifully but peas will be spindly and poor. Another year there will be so many apples that the branches of the trees will almost break under the weight of the fruit.

So it was that Farmer Jones one year had a bumper crop of carrots. When I say he had a bumper crop, I don't mean that he had a fine crop or a very good crop. I mean that his carrots were the biggest, longest, heaviest orange vegetables he had ever seen in his life.

"We shall make a lot of money with this crop," Farmer Jones told his wife, rubbing his hands. But when he went to market, he found that he was not the only one to have a bumper crop of carrots. *Every* farmer he met had piles of the things, and Farmer Jones could not sell his own for any price. The market was full of carrots. No more were needed.

Mr Jones came home in despair. "What are we going to do?" he asked his wife. "We've got three barns of carrots. It will be awful if they simply rot where they lie."

"It won't come to that," said his wife, who was a practical

woman. "I will see if I can use them up in the kitchen."

"Three barns full?" asked the farmer faintly. But as he had no other options, he left it to his wife to do the best she could.

So began the Year of the Carrot. Mrs Jones served them at every meal. She boiled them. She baked them. She broiled them. She steamed them. She sautéed them. She mashed them. She fried them. She grated them.

After three weeks of nobly chomping his way through orange vegetables, the farmer felt he must call a halt. Pushing away his carrot-laden plate, he said, "Dear, I can't face another carrot. If we *must* eat them, can't you disguise them a little?"

Mrs Jones rose to the challenge. She made carrot stews, carrot casseroles and carrot pies. She created carrot risottos and carrot pizzas. She invented a carrot curry and a carrot chow mein. There was no country in the world whose cuisine she did not study to find new you-know-what recipes.

The farmer stood this phase for four weeks. Then he put down his fork and looked at his wife.

"Everything I have eaten for the last month has been orange," he said. "Could we have some ordinary food again?"

Mrs Jones went back to her usual menus, but she had not finished with those carrots. She decided she needed to be even more cunning. Over the next few weeks, the farmer unknowingly ate seventeen carrot cakes, twelve litres of carrot ice cream, forty-eight carrot muffins, twenty litres of carrot tea, six jars of carrot jam, and rather more carrot wine than was good for him. At first he had no idea what he was eating, but when he began to see surprisingly well in the dark, he confronted his wife.

The poor woman confessed that they had eaten little but carrots for several months.

"My dear," said the farmer, "this has got to stop. We'll become ill if we carry on like this. Throw the rest of the carrot cake to the pigs, but whatever you do, don't give them the carrot wine. I still remember what happened after they had the leftover brandy trifle last Christmas."

But mention of the pigs made the farmer begin to feel that he had been very foolish. He tossed a few carrots into the pigsty and watched the pigs munch them. He tried carrots in one form or another on the horses and the goats and the cattle. All of them seemed to enjoy the orange treats.

"Our troubles are over," said the farmer. "All the animals can eat carrots, so we don't have to."

The next-to-last thing I heard about Farmer Jones was that he had emptied one barn of carrots (leaving two to go). The very last thing I heard was that all the animals had marched out of the farmyard and refused to return until the you-know-whats had been taken off the menu. But perhaps that was just a story, and you can't believe everything you read in stories, can you?

The
Christmas
Miracle

Outside, the night was cold, but the stable was full of warm straw and sleeping animals. It was the cosiest place for miles around. When two travellers stumbled into the building and curled up on the straw, the animals were not unduly surprised. They were used to shepherds and cowherds bedding down with them when there was nowhere else to stay. They willingly shifted so there was room for the little donkey that the travellers had brought with them.

"Have you come far?" the ox whispered, so that the human travellers could not hear.

"Yes," replied the donkey. "It has been a long, hard journey. And when we arrived, there was nowhere for us to stay."

Soon there was no sound in the little stable, as the animals and the human visitors all slept soundly in the still night.

But around midnight, there were quiet sounds from the corner where the humans had settled. The animals were woken by a sound they had never heard before. It was the cry of a baby, born that night in the poor stable.

The ox looked across at the tired woman holding the child. She seemed to be surrounded by a golden glow as she rocked the tiny child.

"She could put him in the manger that has our hay in it," the cow whispered to the donkey. "Perhaps you could show them."

The donkey laid his great grey head in the manger, and the lady at once understood him. As he lifted his head, she put her baby carefully in the manger, where he stopped crying and seemed to look around, liking what he saw.

The animals did not want to frighten the little child, so they knelt down in the straw around him. Then they all settled down to sleep once more.

At first the donkey could not understand why it was so hard to go back to sleep. Then he realised that the stable was full of light. Through the cracks in the roof, starlight was streaming, not from the usual stars but from one big star hovering over the building.

It is said that if you go into any stable at midnight on Christmas Eve, you will see the animals kneeling in memory of that special night so many years ago.

Titles in this Series include